GW00468056

THE MAYOR WHO CANCELED CHRISTMAS

A PROVENCE COZY MYSTERY

ANA T. DREW

JULIE CAVALLO INVESTIGATES, BOOK 1

Copyright © 2020 Ana T. Drew

All Rights Reserved.

Editor: Janine Savage

This is a work of fiction.

Names, characters, places and incidents are the product of the author's imagination or are used fictitiously. Any resemblance to actual events, locales, or persons, living or dead, is purely coincidental.

No part of this publication may be reproduced, or transmitted in any form or by any means, electronic or otherwise, without written permission from the author.

CONTENTS

FOREWORD

Provençal mayor Victor Jacquet receives a mystifying note.
Then his small town mounts a rebellion.
And then his entire world implodes.
Some holiday season!
Fortunately for Victor, he never believed in the magic of
Christmas.
Unfortunately for Victor, said magic still believes in him…

**Told from Victor's point of view, this novella stands alone
within the Julie Cavallo Investigates Series.**

Treat yourself to the quirky town of Beldoc, the mayor's
antics, and a gripping mystery!

CHAPTER 1

Dame Fortune so rarely bothers to forewarn us our world is about to turn upside down, that when she does, we always miss the signs.

On this November morning, the mayor of Beldoc Victor Jacquet fixes himself a cup of coffee and plods to the entryway. The howling outside prompts him to wrap his bathrobe tighter around his chest before unlocking the door.

The second it flies open, a powerful gust tears at his face. Squinting, Victor contemplates the show of force that the mistral, Provence's mightiest wind, is giving his town.

Yellow leaves fly high and low, not downward as you'd expect, but horizontally as an irregular contingent of tiny technicolor bats. Wrappers, crumpled sheets of paper, and plastic bags picked up by the howling gale skim alongside the leaves. They have the same unnatural air of purposefulness.

The mistral rattles doors, windows, and fences. The red-striped awning of the grocery store on the corner flaps clamorously. Trees sway, their tops bending in the direction where the army of leaves and debris moves—northwest.

Victor holds an arm over the side of his face. This isn't just a show of force. It's a full-scale military parade!

Blocking the gale with his body, he opens the mailbox and scoops up the mail. Back in his kitchen, he sets the pile down on the table and unfolds his daily copy of *Beldoc Live.* As he reaches for his reading glasses, he notices a small piece of paper on the floor and picks it up.

It's a handwritten note someone slipped in his mailbox. One of its edges is uneven, like it was ripped out of a notebook. Victor notices a greasy smudge. He doesn't recognize the handwriting, and the cryptic message does nothing to help him figure out who the author is. The way it's written, the note has an equal chance to be from a groupie or from a hater.

In light of the fact that Victor is a balding middle-aged man, short and not particularly fit, the latter hypothesis seems more plausible, unless the author is someone between the two extremes. They could be a regular citizen concerned about some wrongdoing they witnessed and coming forward to blow the whistle.

The note reads:

If you'd like us to meet and talk, wear your checkered beret.
Alex D

THE ONLY PERSON in Victor's acquaintance who could call themselves "Alex D" is Alexandra Dalmas, a nurse he briefly dated four years ago, a year after Solange's passing. Everyone in his entourage had been telling him that he'd mourned long enough, and he should try to live again. Solange's best friend and his then-deputy Clothilde badgered him daily. She kept saying Solange wouldn't want him to spend the rest of his days grieving, and she'd want him to meet someone new.

He tried. It didn't work out.

Does Alex want to give it another go?

The note is concise but, reading between the lines, he can deduct a few things. One, the author expects Victor to know who they are. Two, the author is in Beldoc. Three, whoever wrote the note is in a position to see Victor daily. How else would they know if he's wearing his checkered beret?

Alex lived in Arles four years ago. Could she have moved to Beldoc and gotten a job somewhere near Victor's house or town hall where he works? What with Arles being so close to the tiny Beldoc, it would've been an easy move and in tune with the times. These days, the entire country seems to be migrating from bigger to smaller towns.

Has Alex been stalking me?

That doesn't sound like the Alex he dated. Then again, they didn't date long enough to really get to know each other. Besides, people change.

An hour later, Victor leaves the house. The *mairie* is only a fifteen-minute walk away, and it's the only exercise he gets. Over the past month, those fifteen minutes have become a half hour because he's forced to take a detour.

The reason for the detour is a compact fireball of a woman, Magda Ghali. Magda owns a fashionable little shop, Lavender Dream, on rue de l'Andouillette in Beldoc's historic center. Victor's problem isn't Magda herself—even though he's never been a fan—but her fury over something Victor has done. A few weeks ago, he had a public urinal cemented to the sidewalk of Beldoc's liveliest, prettiest street. Right in front of Magda's shop.

To say she didn't take it well would be the understatement of the year. Magda put together a petition and collected hundreds of signatures. She stormed his office at the mairie, called him names and even hurled things at him. She also accused him of nepotism and of misuse of public funds.

Deep inside, Victor doesn't blame her.

He chose the location of the urinal under duress, and now he feels ashamed of himself.

Victor glances at his wristwatch. Having left the house later than usual due to the puzzling note, he's behind schedule. He hates tardiness, so he resolves to take rue de l'Andouillette, hoping that Magda won't see him. Her shop doesn't open to customers until ten, and with the mistral blowing so hard, she won't be standing outside the entrance, puffing on a cigarette. He'll be fine.

Incidentally, the mistral is also the reason Victor isn't wearing his favorite beret. Well, maybe not the only reason. Victor hasn't decided yet if he wants to "meet and talk" with Alex D.

Squinting and blinking to keep his eyes from drying out, he enters rue de l'Andouillette. The wind is weaker here in the center of town, obstructed by all the buildings. Still, Victor's jacket and pants flap against his body, and his thinning hair belts his forehead.

As he passes Lavender Dream, the front door opens a crack.

Magda peeks out, ducking her head in the wind. "Hey, you, corrupt moron! Don't you run away! Face me!"

People turn around. Some stop to watch the show, despite the cutting wind.

"Magda, please, let's not make a scene," he says. "Why don't we discuss it like grown-ups, in my office?"

She points to the bulky, bright red urinal. "Feeling ashamed of your creation, *Monsieur le Maire*? You put that monstrosity in front of my shop with the sole purpose of killing my business!"

"That's not true!"

"Oh yeah?" She steps out and shuts the door behind her. "What else is not true? That your new deputy borrowed a purse, a pair of shoes, a blouse, and a dress from my shop and never paid for those items?"

He lifts his jacket's collar to stop the wind from sliding down his neck. "I know nothing about that."

"Liar!"

"Magda, please, be reasonable. This is not the time or place—"

"You know very well what Blandine Filippi has done, and that I'm suing her!" she yells. "This urinal is retaliation."

"Absolutely not!"

"Absolutely yes! She cornered you and you authorized it."

4

He puts his chin up. "How can you make such outrageous claims?"

As it happens, her claim isn't too outrageous. In fact, it's one hundred percent correct. But Victor will not—cannot—admit it aloud.

Magda scowls. "You were so desperate when Clothilde resigned after being your longtime deputy to run your contender's campaign that you promoted Blandine. And then Blandine came up with the urinal idea and forced your hand by threatening to resign."

He peers at her, impressed by how close her theory is to the truth. The only point she got wrong is that the idea to install the first eco-friendly public urinal in Beldoc was Victor's. But it was Blandine, just like Magda claims, who demanded the urinal stand here on a busy shopping street in front of Magda's window.

Victor had promoted Blandine to deputy mayor back in August for want of better candidates. In hindsight, it was a mistake. Blandine appears to be abusing her newfound status.

When the rumors of her racketeering first reached him, he called her on the carpet. She denied all of it and threatened to quit. Another deputy quitting on him now, in the middle of his reelection campaign, would be catastrophic. He couldn't let it happen.

Magda snaps her fingers in front of his face. "Talk! Look me in the eye and say it isn't true. Say this wasn't Blandine's idea. Say you aren't helping her bully me into dropping the lawsuit?"

"I am not," he says firmly. "The urinal was my idea."

Formally, both statements are true, which is why Victor was able to make them as he stared into Magda's heavily painted eyes.

He turns on his heel and strides away from the shop owner spewing flavorful epithets after him.

Merde!

He really doesn't need this now in the middle of a

campaign that's turning out to be his hardest since his first one thirty years back.

Wait, what if Magda wrote the mysterious note?

What if it's a trap? A gossiper extraordinaire, it's likely Magda has heard about Alex, the only woman Victor dated since his wife's passing. So, she figured she'd write him a note signed "Alex D." Her plan is to lure him somewhere secluded, kidnap him, and hold him captive until he orders the removal of the urinal.

Victor shakes his head. *What a ludicrous theory!*

Why look for convoluted explanations when the obvious one is also the most plausible? Alex Dalmas wrote the note, hoping to rekindle their relationship.

One of these days, Victor will need to decide if he wants to give it a try. Alex seemed like a good person, and far from unpleasant to look at. He wasn't ready back then and wasn't willing to put in the effort to make it work. But he's in a better place now. Four years have passed. He still misses Solange every day, but less acutely. What if Alex can make him happy again?

Quit fooling yourself!

The relationship failed the first time around. Why would it succeed on take two?

Besides, happiness is obnoxious.

When so many things are wrong with the world, how can anyone make merry? With all the wars, injustice, suffering, environmental catastrophes and deadly viruses, how can anyone party and laugh? How dare they feel carefree? How dare they seek joy?!

The familiar righteous anger at human callousness fills the aching hollow in Victor's heart.

He perks up, welcoming his old friend. There's so much comfort in that anger! That sharp awareness of human misery and of the world's looming collapse makes for the best tonic, always has. It's what drives Victor.

It's what makes him taller than the gung-ho fools.

CHAPTER 2

S hielding his face with his arm, Victor keeps going.

All shops are closed, even the bakeries that should already be open at this time. The streets are empty save for the people heading into work. No one halts, be it for a cup of coffee or a chat. With their heads down and their collars up, they troop on, hoping to be indoors by the time the wind gets stronger.

And the mistral always gets stronger, no matter the season. But its twisted humor gets downright perverse during the winter months when it chases the clouds away. By doing so, it reveals an unfriendly sun that makes the wind's bite sting more instead of warming the air.

Victor turns the last corner before the finish line. A light post with hooks that hold four baskets filled with multicolored flowers catches his eye. One of the baskets has fallen off its hook. Victor tries to hang it back up, but part of it is broken and the basket drops to the ground again. He leaves it alone. The municipal landscaper will fix it.

Hopefully, there won't be too much breakage when the mistral is done with Beldoc. The town's treasury is in no shape to advance funds for any major repairs.

Victor slows down before the underground parking

garage to make sure a car isn't driving out. There isn't any. Instead, he spots Karl, his dog, and another hobo. They're huddled on the narrow walkway along the exit ramp with their backs against the concrete wall amid cigarette butts and empty beer cans.

The three of them are wrapped in tattered, dirty blankets —one for each human and two for the dog.

"Karl" isn't the tramp's real name. Everyone calls him that because of his long, thick, sliver-white hair, combed back into a low ponytail. It gives him a vaguely Karl Lagerfeld-like appearance if one ignores the rest of his unkempt appearance.

Garage ramps aren't Karl's usual stomping grounds. He favors spots in the open, where there's light and a better chance of people noticing his coin cup. He seeks shelter only when the weather gets really bad.

"Bonjour, Karl!" Victor calls as he walks by the fragrant group.

He struggles to not pinch his nose.

A smile appears on the tramp's weather-beaten face. "Bonjour, Monsieur le Maire!"

Victor averts his gaze from Karl's missing front teeth—at least two of them—and looks at his companion.

Karl's new buddy is a lanky youth, somewhere between seventeen and twenty-one. Victor would've been able to determine his age with more precision if his face were less grimy. And his hair less green.

The kid is a punk. He sports all the requisite attributes—a mohawk haircut, tight jeans, a band T-shirt, a tattered leather jacket, pins and buttons with anti-capitalist slogans, studs and spikes, and of course, army boots. If somewhere on the Internet there exists an inventory of the nonconformist young rebel, he'll check every box.

Quickening his pace, Victor crosses the *Place de la Mairie*, and practically runs up the stairs of the town hall. It isn't only the wind propelling him today. He's about to make a big announcement to his staff.

Twenty minutes later, the municipal team is gathered in the meeting room, notepads and pens on the table, and steaming mugs in their hands.

Victor squares his shoulders. "As of today, we are no longer radical deconstructivists, but radical environmentalists!"

The staff stare at him, their mouths agape.

His deputy Blandine is the first to voice the mood in the room. "What the heck, Victor? We've started distributing campaign flyers and gluing posters on walls. I have personally—"

"Radical deconstructivism doesn't inspire the masses anymore," he says, interrupting. "You want the truth? It's been losing steam since the nineties."

Sandrine Krauss, the head of urban planning, lifts her eyes from her mug. "And you realized it just now?"

"I've been aware of the hemorrhage for a while," Victor admits. "But I didn't see an alternative."

Carefully, Sandrine sets her mug on the table. "How is environmentalism an alternative? It wants to save the planet from humanity. Deconstructivism is about saving humanity from itself!"

"You can be an eco-activist without hating humanity," Victor counters. "Besides, we've got to be pragmatic if we want to win this election." He surveys his staffers. "If you want to keep your jobs."

That shuts Sandrine up.

Victor's lifetime secretary, Chantal, launches into her landmark Headshake of Dissent. It starts as a mild tremor, escalates to a rhythmic side-to-side wobble, and finally becomes a vigorous swing.

"It would be a betrayal of our ideals, of your father's legacy!" she says.

"It's a matter of survival," Victor snaps. "Go green or go home."

She purses her lips, eyes welling up.

9

Victor softens his tone. "Chantal, we don't have to turn our backs on deconstructivism. We'll wear green camouflage over our scarlet hearts and continue the fight!"

"What do you propose we do, concretely?" Blandine asks.

Thank you! "Excellent question! For starters, we'll change our name and repurpose our slogans and branding."

"I can run point on that," she offers.

He gives her a thumbs-up and turns to Chantal. "I'm sure we can recycle some of my father's brilliant speeches and manifestos. His legacy will live on. We'll just swap 'structural systems' for 'eco-systems,' and the rest will fall into place."

The male staffers speak up at last.

"Radical deconstructivism never fully recovered from the fall of the Berlin Wall," Fred says. "That event gave people false hopes for a brighter future."

"Today, people are just as scared as they were at the height of the Cold War," Karim chimes in. "Back then it was the nukes, and now it's the virus and plastic in the oceans. People are sad and counting down to doomsday. We can use that."

"We can rage like before, but no one will ridicule us anymore!" Damien gushes. "They'll applaud!"

One after the other, they back Victor's idea. As they scramble to stress the benefits of the pivot, Victor can't help but notice how much easier it is to command men than women. Underneath their air of docility and ready smiles, women are rebels at heart. They're the true anarchists! They're always the first to defy a leader and the last to rally behind him.

His estranged sister, Marlene, is the perfect example.

Growing up, she never showed the kind of enthusiasm Victor had for their parents' ideals, their life's work, and their fight. While he spent every spare hour of his teenage years handing out pamphlets and going to rallies, she did none of that. She never spoke during the late-night gatherings in their house when everyone got worked up about smashing the system and building a better world.

Victor will never forget the fiery energy of those nights.

He was a part of it, body and soul. But Marlene always had that detached look on her face. She'd sit in the corner, quiet as a mouse with her nose in a book or in needlework. She'd refuse to offer an opinion, a nod, or any kind of reaction to the heated debates. When asked if she agreed or disagreed with a viewpoint, she'd say she didn't know.

And then, the day she turned eighteen, she packed a suitcase and took the train to a Benedictine monastery near Tours. First, it was a spiritual retreat. Then it turned into an aspirancy. And then she took her vows and became a nun in one of the strictest French orders that required she never leave her convent.

Talk about female betrayals!

Between Marlene and Clothilde, Victor has had his share of betrayals. Marlene's hurt worse, no doubt. It wasn't just her choosing a guy who died on a cross two thousand years ago over her family and their noble cause. Her life choice was a slap on their parents' faces. Victor would never forgive Marlene for that. Even though she was allowed to call her family and receive visitors, he cut off all contact. *Maman* and *Papa* did the same.

Ah, if only I could snub Clothilde in the same way without appearing immature!

Papa died ten years ago without having spoken to Marlene in two decades.

Seven years ago, Maman suffered a stroke. On her hospital bed between life and death, she managed to convey she wanted to talk to Marlene. Against his better judgment, Victor looked up the monastery's phone number and called.

"Ask if she's still there," Maman breathed.

He relayed the question.

"Yes, she is," the front desk nun answered.

He reported the information to Maman.

While he waited for someone to fetch Marlene, out in the vineyard picking grapes, Maman passed away.

Victor ended the call. In his heart, he knew that it was the disappointment that her daughter was still wasting her life away as a nun that finished Maman off.

He didn't pick up when the convent called back.

CHAPTER 3

The mistral stopped yesterday, after tormenting Beldoc for five straight days.

The sky has been overcast since then. The weather is warmer, and the Christmas madness is upon the town once again.

Victor drags himself out of bed, washes, shaves, climbs into his most official-looking suit, and swallows two cups of coffee. He glances at the handwritten note on the table, which he still hasn't done anything about. Pushing it aside, he trudges out of the kitchen.

He doesn't want to go to work. This morning, he doesn't feel like leaving his house at all.

But he must.

The reason Victor wishes he could take a day off today is the municipal council meeting that awaits him. Not the meeting in itself, but the third item on its agenda— Preparations for Christmas.

That alone is unpleasant enough. Ever since he can remember, Victor has disliked Christmastime. His parents believed it was a pointless extravaganza, the pinnacle of unbridled consumption that goes with the Western way of life. Victor believes that, too.

Stopping in front of the entryway mirror, Victor tells

himself he should refrain from using the verb "believe." Beliefs are for the superstitious, irrational crowd that loves Christmas. They are for the indoctrinated bunch like Marlene. His views have nothing to do with the cheap joy promoted by corporations to sell more goods. His ideas, his parents' ideas, are rooted in materialism, not in consumerism.

Victor adjusts his tie and slings the tricolor mayoral sash across his chest. Even though he wants to, he can't wear his checkered beret today.

Three days ago, he made up his mind about Alex and left the house with the beret on his head. He'd barely made it to the corner of the street when the wind snatched his favorite cap and threw it under the busy traffic.

Victor managed to retrieve it, but it was deformed and smeared with dirt, grease, and tar. Holding it away from his clothes between his thumb and forefinger, he took it back home. On closer inspection, he found no tears. There was hope that Beldoc's best dry cleaner could restore it to a wearable state.

On a heavy sigh, Victor opens the door and walks out.

This year, the dreaded Christmas planning meeting is going to be particularly unpleasant. The traitress Clothilde and his challenger Rose Tassy, both members of the municipal Events Committee, will be there. They'll hate the news he'll give them. There will be a confrontation. Things might get ugly.

Victor takes a detour to the mairie. The last thing he needs before the inevitable clash at the council meeting is a face-off with Magda.

His circuitous route takes him to the riverfront past one of Karl's haunts by the bridge. Victor keeps an eye out for Karl and the punk, but he can't see them.

Clothilde and Rose, on the other hand, are all he can see when the council sitting starts.

Both ladies are already in the meeting room when he walks in. These proceedings being open to the public, Rose has rounded up a few fans, including her friend Sarah Owen, her pastry chef granddaughter Julie Cavallo and—*darn it!*—Magda Ghali.

This does not bode well.

Victor takes his seat and opens the manila envelope in front of him. Efficient as ever, Chantal has prepared enough of them for each attendee to have one. The envelope contains the minutes of the last sitting, the agenda of the current one, and all the relevant documents.

To Victor's surprise, Magda and the rest of the troublemakers keep quiet while the council discusses the first two agenda items.

After Blandine introduces the third, Victor takes the floor. "This year, we're going to change things up. There will be no Christmas tree on Beldoc's Place de la Mairie or on any other square."

The room gasps. Then, shocked whats and whys hit him from everywhere.

"I have a good reason for the ban!" Victor shouts over multiple voices.

The room falls silent, curious to hear it.

"My team and I do not wish to encourage consumerism," Victor says. "And we want an eco-friendly holiday season."

"In what way is our cherished Christmas tree an impediment to that?" Sarah asks.

Victor adjusts his tie. "Well, you see the tree encourages compulsive gift buying. People acquire useless items just to have something to put under the tree."

"Are you going to ban Christmas trees in private homes, too?" Rose asks, her tone laced with sarcasm.

I wish I could!

"Of course not," Victor replies. "But my team and I will discourage them on the radio, in *Beldoc Live* and when speaking in schools."

"That's called indoctrination of young minds!" Sarah blasts. "Right out of Hitler's textbook!"

Victor bangs the table. "I will not be compared to Hitler, madame!"

"Then don't use his methods," she retorts.

"All I want is to make our town greener," Victor says in a placating tone. "I want more vegetation, more living trees in Beldoc. I don't want living trees slaughtered in the name of consumerism! Whether you like it or not, we're ditching the Christmas tree."

"But what about the spiritualism of its meaning?" Rose asks. "To many of us, it symbolizes the birth of Jesus. You aren't qualified to deny us that celebration!"

Victor glares at his rival.

Really, Rose? You're a former hippie who believes in karma and never goes to church. You aren't qualified to talk about Jesus!

He opens his mouth to say just that, when Clothilde butts in. "You know what the Christmas tree also stands for, Victor? Family. Friendship. Human connection. Love. You want to cancel those, too?"

Victor redirects his scowl at her.

What a sucker punch. That was low, Clothilde, even for you!

She knows better than anyone in this room how lonely he's been since Solange and his parents passed. She knows he has no real friends.

"Anyhow, it doesn't matter what the Christmas tree represents," he says at length. "There's no money to pay for it this year. The municipality has used that budget line for… er… a town planning project. Discussion closed."

Rose claps a hand to her mouth. "You sneaky, scheming, shameless ruffian! You didn't… Did you?"

She knows. She figured it out, the witch!

Victor chews on his pencil, refusing to respond.

The council members, staffers, and citizens look from Rose to him and back.

"What?" many ask. "What is this about?"

"The urinal," Rose says without taking her eyes off him. "He spent the Christmas tree budget on purchasing and installing that god-awful public urinal in front of Magda's shop."

Something hurtles across the room, like a frisbee, and smashes into Victor's face. It's an unopened manila envelope. Victor swears and rubs his sore nose. It doesn't seem broken.

Like a shark smelling blood, Magda draws her daggerlike, red nails and launches herself at him.

Before she's had a chance to scratch Victor's chest, Blandine slams her purse on Magda's head. The ladies yelp and grab handfuls of each other's hair. Magda kicks Blandine's shin. Blandine steps on Magda's foot. Bawling, Magda lets go of Blandine's hair and rips her silk blouse down the front.

"Aaaargh!" Blandine swings to punch Magda. "That cost a fortune, you dumb cow!"

Magda blocks the blow. "Serves you right, thief!"

They grapple with each other and tumble down.

Rose, Julie, Sandrine and a few men rush to the pair who are now rolling on the floor. They pull the determined wrestlers apart and drag them to the opposite corners of the room.

Victor rises to his feet. "This council meeting is over! We'll discuss the remaining two items in January."

People fidget and wriggle but stay put, clearly too entertained to leave just yet.

Chantal rushes to Victor's side. "Mesdames, Messieurs, it's truly over! Please go home!"

Without saying another word, she stretches both arms toward the doors on each side, the way flight attendants show the emergency exits during the safety demo.

"Merry Christmas, everyone!" she cries as the reluctant attendees shuffle to the doors.

CHAPTER 4

Today is Monday, which means Magda's shop is closed.

It also means Victor can safely go to Tatiana's Brasserie on rue de l'Andouillette for lunch. He likes her simple, cheap food better than the fancier fares served at Le Grand Comptoir. But he's been staying away from the brasserie since October, loath to be yelled at in public—yet again—by the infuriated owner of Lavender Dream.

At ten to one, Victor grabs his coat and heads down the stairs of the mairie. He isn't wearing his checkered beret. It's at the dry cleaner's with a bleak prognosis and little chance of a full recovery.

Quelle poisse!

If Victor believed in God or spirits or anything supernatural, he'd say a prayer now. He really did love that beret. Besides, if Alex is watching him, she'll think that by not wearing it, he's saying that he isn't interested in giving their relationship another go. She'll back off.

That said, Victor doesn't believe in second chances as far as relationships are concerned. Nor does he anticipate that anything good can come from meeting with Alex. But he's a little curious to see if she's still as curvy and bubbly as she was four years ago. At the time, he was still raw from

Solange's passing, and Alex's peppiness aggravated him. But since then much water has passed under the bridges on the Rhône.

Not to mention that it's bad manners to ignore a lady's invitation!

Victor smiles to himself. Chivalry is so deeply ingrained in French men that even a lifelong radical deconstructivist raised by lifelong radical deconstructivists carries the bias.

Crossing the Place de la Marie, Victor passes a food truck. He nods hello to the vendor who waves back. The area around the truck smells different today. Victor realizes that the usual chocolaty smell of Nutella crepes has been supplanted by the characteristic bouquet of warm red wine, cinnamon, and orange. It reeks of Christmas.

The whole town stinks of Christmas. There are garlands, wreaths, and ornaments everywhere. Strings of glittering lights zigzag between buildings and cascade down shop windows. Sidewalk trees are wrapped in shimmering gauzes that give them a fairy-tale-like look.

To Victor's dismay, Beldoc feels just as Christmassy this year as it did last year, despite the absence of the big Christmas tree in the center of the Place de la Mairie.

Speaking of which, some folks are seriously upset about it.

But Victor stands his ground. Over the past two weeks, he's received countless individuals and groups, all trying to persuade him to change his mind. He replied to each and every one that their mayor, a radical environmentalist, will have no part in killing a living tree just so humans can decorate it.

Patiently, he explained to them that the Christmas spirit is a fabrication. It's a clever stratagem, he said, to get people into an optimistic, festive mood. He argued that the ritual of gift-giving isn't about love and generosity, but about retail and economy. The sole purpose of the holiday season, he told them, is to get people to spend their hard-earned cash on things they don't need.

Hopefully, he was able to make them see Christmas through his eyes.

Victor walks into Tatiana's Brasserie and settles at his usual table by the window.

"Bonjour, Monsieur le Maire!" she cries out, rushing to him with a menu.

Greeting her, he sweeps his hand around the room. "Congratulations on the absence of garish Christmas ornaments! You're the only business owner in town to resist the hysteria."

"Oh no, I love that stuff," she says. "But I don't have the heart this year."

He frowns. "What's wrong?"

"It's been rough." Her generous bust heaves. "I'm selling the brasserie."

"What? I knew nothing about it! Why?"

"The place doesn't attract enough customers to be profitable," she says.

"But I eat here often!"

"You're in the minority, Monsieur le Maire." She skews a feeble smile. "People find this place too generic, too uncool. And they want fancier food."

"Can they afford fancier food?"

"The ones that still eat out regularly, the loafers-with-tassels crowd, can," she says.

"But not the yellow-vest folks," he counters. "They are your customers, are they not?"

She nods. "Except, they've grown too poor even for my ten-euro menu. Many have lost their jobs or buying power. They don't make enough for extras anymore."

Sad but true.

"What about the tourists?" he asks.

"My brasserie is too shabby to attract them." She shakes her head woefully. "And, since I haven't turned a profit in a while, I can't afford to have it redone. No bank would lend me money."

He pouts in anger. "The vicious circle of capitalism!"

She nods.

"You're probably the last working-class food joint in this town," he laments. "The rest are chic neo-bistros and gluten-free nonsense."

She glances at the pastry shop across the street with the sign Julie's Gluten-Free Delights. "Yeah."

Victor follows her gaze. "I could have *steak-frites* and beer at your place for the price of a tiny macaron at hers!"

He knows he's exaggerating but it's to make a point.

"Well, the thing is…" Tatiana plays with her apron strings. "You know, with the expenses going up and the customers making themselves scarce, I've had to raise my prices."

You too, Brutus?

She hands him the menu.

He scans it. "You doubled almost all of the prices since last week!"

"Believe me, Victor, I had no choice." Her eyes tear up. "And it didn't even move the needle! Which is why I'm forced to sell the place."

Wincing, he orders today's special and turns to gaze out the window.

Things are suddenly happening on the street.

Karl, his dog and the punk, neither of whom Victor saw in two weeks, are setting up camp under the oak tree.

From one of his bags, Karl pulls a *jambon-beurre* someone must've given him. He breaks it into three equal parts, one of which he gives to the punk and the other to his happy mongrel. The punk opens his dirty backpack and fishes out a bottle of water. He hands it to Karl who takes a swig before pouring some into a paper cup for the dog.

They're having a picnic!

A couple of meters away from them, another group has gathered in front of Julie's shop. This one consists of women only and includes the traitor Clothilde, the mayoral candidate Rose, her floppy-eared dog, and a woman in her mid-thirties. They all talk animatedly. The thirtysomething reminds Victor of Rose back when she was a teacher at his school and he had a crush on her.

She must be one of Rose's many granddaughters.

Speaking of whom, Julie steps out of the shop carrying a tray with two steaming paper cups and two croissants.

The thirtysomething reaches for a croissant, but Rose swats her hand and points to Karl. The woman tilts her head upward in an "oh-I-see" gesture.

Julie carries the coffee and croissants over to the picnickers. The thirtysomething follows her.

Victor heard from his secretary who heard from Magda that the shops on this block have a deal with Karl. He stays away from the urinal until they close for business. In return, they supply coffee and treats.

The problem, again according to Magda via Chantal, isn't Karl. It's all those random men who use the contraption throughout the day.

Does Victor regret submitting to Blandine's blackmail and installing the urinal here?

Of course, he does!

Did he have a choice?

Nope, he didn't.

The thirtysomething engages the punk in a conversation. They both smile and even laugh at times. Then she says something that seems to annoy him. The kid's expression tightens. He turns away from the woman and pets Karl's dog.

Rose catches Victor watching them.

She waves to her gang, pointing out the brasserie. Before Victor can say knife, they file into Tatiana's.

She hurries to the door to welcome them. "Rose! Julie! Clothilde!" She turns to the thirtysomething. "Madame, bonjour!"

After she directs them to a table, the women remove their coats, hang them on the backs of their chairs, and sit down. Rose's dog settles under the table.

Tatiana moves the menu board with today's specials

written in chalk closer to them, before retreating to the kitchen.

Sipping his water, Victor steals a glance at Rose.

Underneath her well-cut tweed jacket, she's wearing a T-shirt that reads *Make Your Queen Your Mayor!* Her companions all have large pins with campaign slogans.

Rose thinks she's being clever, referencing her status as Queen of Beldoc. Traditionally, Provençal towns elect beautiful young women as their "queens." The charming demoiselles' task—against a small allowance—is to act as the town's ambassador to the outside world.

This summer, when the Queen elections were held across Provence, the town of Beldoc had a shortage of candidates. To be more exact, there were none. Apparently, the pretty young Beldocian women thought that the prestige of being a queen and the size of the allowance, didn't make up for the time and effort they'd be expected to dedicate to the job over the next four years.

Thus, Beldoc had to drop the age threshold. A few retired ladies applied. Rose Tassy won the contest at seventy-five years old.

Tatiana serves Victor's canard confit before darting to Rose's table. "Ready to order?"

They are. And they do.

Rose points to the thirtysomething. "Remember Veronique, my oldest granddaughter?"

"I do!" Tatiana looks at her. "Where do you live these days?"

"In Montreal," Veronique says. "I'm here to spend Christmas with Rose and my sisters."

Tatiana smiles. "The Cavallo Quartet."

"The Quartet will be here in full in a few days when my twin arrives from Paris," Julie says.

The Quartet should've been a Solo!

Big families are the scourge of the earth. They cause overpopulation, which causes overconsumption, which leads to a shortage of resources, which results in conflicts and wars.

23

Uplifted by his legitimate wrath at people's irresponsible behaviors, Victor focuses on his main course.

When his post-meal espresso arrives, Clothilde turns up at his table. "Can we talk?"

"I have nothing to say to a turncoat colluding with my enemies to overthrow me!"

She gawks, visibly taken aback by the fervency of his outburst. "I was Solange's best friend since childhood," she finally says. "Hear me out for her sake!"

He snorts. "You have a *Rose for Mayor* pin."

She lowers her voice. "Please, Vic!"

"All right, whatever. Say what you have to say."

"I still miss her, you know?" She wraps her wool cardigan tighter around her chest. "I can only imagine how it is for you."

"Some wounds never heal."

"True." She hesitates before adding, "But you have a sister. Don't you think about her sometimes? Don't you wonder how she's faring?"

He shrugs. "She's a nun."

"Is that such a terrible thing?"

"To me, it is."

"Hey, you know what? It's Christmastime! Let some love into your life, Vic! You could reconnect—"

"You walked out on me midcampaign to join my rival," he says, interrupting her. "You should be too ashamed to look me in the eye, let alone give me advice on how to live my life."

"I'm sorry," she whispers.

He picks up his cup and turns away.

CHAPTER 5

It's already dark when Victor steps out of the town hall.

A dense, boisterous crowd has filled Beldoc's main square, Place de la Mairie, which now hosts a Christmas market. Nearly everyone is carrying a paper bag with gifts they've just purchased. Most marketgoers are families with young children. But there are also groups of laughing youths, elderly couples holding hands, people with dogs, and people by themselves.

They all navigate between rows of wooden chalet-styled booths, their openings trimmed with blinking lights. The wares sold include costume jewelry, scarves and shawls in vibrant colors, essential oils, fragrances and soaps, cosmetics, and treats.

An overhead stereo alternates between folk songs and Christmas carols, reinforcing the festive ambiance.

Victor passes the spot in the center of the square where the big Christmas tree would typically stand. The petition launched by Rose to make him change his mind has garnered an insane amount of signatures within days, but he hasn't caved in. No more ritual tree sacrifices on my watch, he announced in an interview in *Beldoc Live* and on the radio. Deal with it, losers!

That last bit, he didn't say aloud.

A booth selling *santons* reminds Victor that the decorated tree isn't the only symbol of Christmas. The hand-painted terracotta figurines are definitely another one. At least here, in Provence.

Traditionally used to re-create the Nativity scene, the figurines are an unintended by-product of the French Revolution. When the *Terreur* shut down the churches, killing priests and driving religion underground, a reactionary potter in Marseilles came up with the brilliant idea to shrink the Christmas crib.

Then, Napoleon restored the Catholic Church, and the santons lost their *raison d'être*. They should've disappeared. They are the perfect example of obsolete objects that should've never made it into the present century. Yet, somehow, they did.

Needless to say, there's no room for them in the town hall as long as Victor is the mayor of Beldoc! Perhaps he should go further and ban Baby Jesus and the Virgin Mary from the market. The others can stay. Not all santons are about the Nativity. Some represent characters from an idealized Provençal village.

Victor peers, trying to identify them in the display.

Here we have a *pâtissière* wearing a chef's hat and a white lace wrap around her shoulders. And here's a miller, carrying a sack of wheat. There's the *ravi*—a very popular character—basically, the village idiot. Victor also spots the pretty shepherdess with a lamb, the less pretty fishmonger in a full Arlesienne costume, the blind man, and the chestnut seller.

Satisfied with his inventory, he turns his back to the santons and heads toward the food stalls. Some of them have canvas awnings, others just tablecloths, but they're invariably red. Victor's mouth twists. Even more so than green, red has become the official color of Christmas. Why? Because corporations have figured out that it excites and encourages people to buy more.

A honeyed, mouthwatering smell of Spanish churros wafts from one of the food stalls. Others boast the complete

Thirteen Christmas Sweets of Provence. Other vendors sell drinks—mulled wine, cider, tea, coffee, hot chocolate, and sodas.

Cursing himself for his weakness, Victor slinks to the nearest food stall where he buys a deliciously fragrant mulled wine. With the heat of the cup warming his hands, he picks his way to the other side of the square. But something catches his eye.

Speaking of chestnut sellers! Next to the children's merry-go-round, he notices a familiar face behind the roaster. Said roaster consists of a hot plate placed over a fire that burns inside a metal drum with ventilation holes in it. Another archaic object that shouldn't have survived into this century!

"Chaud les marrons!" the vendor yells.

The guy barking every French chestnut man's tagline is none other than Karl. Considerably cleaner than usual with a crisp white apron around his hips and a Santa hat on his head, he seems to be having a blast.

His dog is at his feet, sitting on its haunches and keeping an eye on things. Its head has been shaved but for a spiky strip running between his ears and down his neck. The hairstyle is a miniature mohawk in the same bright green color as the punk's.

Karl follows Victor's gaze. "How do you like Harley's cut?"

"It's eye-catching," Victor says. "Your new friend's creation?"

Karl grins. "He says I have style, and so should Harley."

"Except he fashioned Harley's after his own, not yours."

"I don't mind! And let me tell you, the kid is real good with his hands. Not just for styling, but for all sorts of stuff. Fixes things like a pro."

"Where is he, by the way?" Victor asks. "Why isn't he selling chestnuts with you to make some cash?"

"He found other kids to hang out with. They must be at the squat, playing music."

Victor narrows his eyes. "What squat?"

Realizing he said too much, Karl swallows before adding in a hot whisper, "Monsieur le Maire, it isn't someone's summer house, or anything like that. I promise!"

"What is it, then?"

"I know that the building has been abandoned for years," Karl says. "An inheritance dispute, I'm told."

Victor knows that building and the story behind it. "It's one of those ugly family feuds that turn into a legal imbroglio with no end in sight, and a lot of money filling lawyers' pockets."

"Exactly!"

Karl fills a paper cone with freshly cracked chestnuts and hands it to a woman in exchange for two euros.

"By the way," he says, pocketing the money, "someone reported the squat to the gendarmes last week, and Capitaine Adinian showed up to check on the kids. He said they could stay through the winter on the condition they respect fire safety and don't do drugs."

"I doubt that's what he said."

Karl signs himself. "Cross my heart!"

"So, those kids hate the idea of work so much they'd rather live in filth than look for a job. How typical for his generation!"

"It's against the True Punk philosophy to work for money," Karl explains. "They call it 'selling out' to the consumerist society."

"How do they get by?"

"DIY, dumpster diving, and panhandling." Karl smiles a toothless smile. "Like me, basically."

The anti-consumerist part, Victor supports wholeheartedly. But the radical deconstructivist in him cannot condone the rejection of ennobling labor by Karl and the punk.

"What's wrong with being a proletarian?" he asks, his tone boorish.

Karl points his chin down to his hands as he stirs chestnuts. "Hey, don't ask me, I'm a proletarian!"

Pff, smartass! This is the first time he's worked in a decade. Victor bids Karl goodbye.

As he nears the edge of the square, he catches sight of the punk, talking with the two Cavallo girls—Julie and Veronique. He pretends to be browsing some items displayed on a stand and listens.

"Do you guys have sleeping pads or mattresses?" Julie asks him.

"There were old mattresses when my buddies cracked the squat, but they got rid of them."

"Why?"

"Because every crust punk knows, you don't sleep on a used mattress," the kid explains. "Nine times out of ten, it's full of bed bugs and yucky germs."

From the corner of his eye, Victor can see a fleeting smile touch Veronique's lips as she glances at the punk's grimy backpack.

"Hey, you know what?" Julie says. "Our grandma Rose has a dozen or so spare mats!"

"How come?" he asks.

"Her former doga students left them behind."

"What's doga?"

"It's yoga practiced with dogs," Veronique explains. "Grandma is a doga instructor."

"So, yeah, she doesn't know what to do with those mats," Julie says.

His eyes light up. "I hate putting my sleeping bag on the hard floor. It's so freaking uncomfortable! The others don't mind as much I do, but they'd be thrilled about those pads. Can we have them?"

"Absolutely!" Julie pulls out her phone. "Give me the address and a convenient time, and we'll swing by."

He gives her the requested details, which she thumbs into her phone.

"With regard to the other matter," Veronique says. "Rose has an idea."

He grins, dipping his head to one side. "I'm listening."

Julie looks around, spots Victor, and nudges her sister and the punk away.

What other matter?

They're too far away now and whispering, so it's impossible to make out what is being discussed. But, whatever it is, the Cavallo sisters are obviously trying to get the punk to do something for them. Or, more likely, for their grandmother.

That's why they offered the mats. That's why they're so nice to him.

But what in hell are they after?

The kid is a traveler. Crust punks are always on the move, train hopping and hitchhiking. It isn't like he's going to stick around long enough to cast a vote for Rose! Besides, he isn't a registered voter in Beldoc. Are they hoping he'll persuade Karl to vote for Rose? As if the hobo ever bothered to do his civic duty!

And even if he did, that's a lot of effort for one, very uncertain, vote.

No, Rose must be cooking something up. That woman always has a secret agenda. She wouldn't be Rose Tassy if she didn't. There must be something she hopes to achieve by helping the punk, even if Victor cannot fathom what that could possibly be.

Don't you worry, Rose, I'll find out! And I'll thwart you!

CHAPTER 6

This morning, Victor is in a bit of a hurry to get to his office. Still, he takes the longer route to avoid Magda's verbal and physical assaults.

By the river, he spies Karl and his dog. Unlike his usual aimless gait, Karl is treading with an expression of intent on his face and a certain energy in his step. It's clear he's going to a specific place. A charity handout? The chestnut stand? Is Karl able to work several days in a row?

The punk isn't with him. He must be still asleep at his squat.

Victor walks faster. It won't do to arrive late to the monthly staff meeting! There are bosses who drag their feet on purpose as a statement of who's in charge. Victor isn't that kind of boss. He believes in leading by example.

Still, even the risk of falling short of his own standards won't make him venture onto rue de l'Andouillette.

Today's detour takes Victor past the gendarmerie. Outside the main entrance, he spies the punk and Capitaine Adinian.

Uh-oh.

The kid must've pilfered something. Or tagged an unauthorized wall. Or, maybe, Adinian busted the squat first thing in the morning and caught him doing drugs. Even though the punk doesn't have the characteristic wild, shifty-eyed and sunken-cheeked look of a junkie, he could still be an occasional user. It's something that goes with the gutter lifestyle.

To Victor's surprise, instead of nudging his catch in through the main entrance, Adinian leads him around the building.

Intrigued, Victor follows.

The capitaine and the kid stop in the back of the courtyard, close to a group of builders in coveralls. The refacing of the gendarmerie's rear façade completed now, the contractor is dismantling the scaffolding and cleaning up the site.

Adinian points to plywood sheets stacked by the wall. "They were used to board up the building while under renovation."

He beckons to one of the builders who jogs toward them.

"We're talking about the plywood," Adinian says to the builder.

The man nods. "Yeah, since the company's next project doesn't start before mid-January, we'll be taking the plywood to the municipal dump."

The punk goes closer to inspect the sheets.

"What do you think?" Adinian asks him.

The punk grins. "They'll do."

For what?

"I've got to go," Adinian says, checking his watch. "See you later, then."

The kid makes the rock 'n' roll sign of the horns with both hands. "Cool!"

Victor tears out before he's discovered.

As he runs the short distance to the mairie, panting, he remembers how Karl said the kid was skilled with his hands, and that DIY was a part of "the punk philosophy." *That's it!* The squatters must've mentioned a project to Adinian on his first visit. Maybe they'd like to build a table or a settee for their squat. Then this morning, the capitaine saw the plywood destined for the dump, and realized the punks could reuse some of it.

What an unexpectedly eco-friendly gesture for a cop!

With an approving smile, Victor climbs the stairs of the mairie.

≈

AT ONE IN THE AFTERNOON, Victor and his team leave their offices for lunch at Le Grand Comptoir, as they always do after a staff meeting. The restaurant is much more expensive than Tatiana's Brasserie, but it offers two advantages. First, it's right on the town hall square, so they don't have to rush. The second benefit is the low to negligible odds of Hurricane Magda.

Victor's secretary Chantal has reserved a long table by the window, the one they always take.

As they dig into their starters, Victor notices some commotion in the part of the square free from the Christmas market stalls. Grateful for the unobstructed view, he puts on his distance glasses and peers out the window.

A gendarmerie van has pulled up by the curb, just outside of the pedestrian zone. Adinian and Isnard emerge from the front seats and open the tailgate. Out jump the punk, the dog and Karl.

The Cavallo sisters—Julie, Veronique, and the youngest whose name escapes Victor—come out of nowhere and beeline toward them. All three are saddled with big duffel bags. Warm greetings are exchanged. The men point to the van. The women crane their necks to sneak a peek, and then show the men the contents of their bags. Everyone gloves up.

It looks like they're all in on something, getting ready to act. *Doing what?*

The dog wags its tail and bounds around them, infected by the excitement they give off.

What the hell is going on?

The punk says something to the gendarmes. They go to the van and haul out three shipping pallets and a big toolbox. The punk places the pallets on top of one another and screws them together with a power screwdriver. Julie retrieves a set of synthetic turf squares from her duffel bag. She secures those to the top pallet with double-sided tape.

The youngest Cavallo sister plants herself in the center of the "clearing" and waves to the others. When she gets their attention, she points down and shouts, *Here!*

Now Victor has an inkling of what's going on.

His staffers have now abandoned their soups and salads to follow the events unfolding outside. Passersby and market-goers stop to watch. More people assemble, whispering to each other and smiling as they catch on.

Suddenly, everyone in the square is looking in the direction of the van. Victor follows their gazes, and his eyes widen at what he sees.

CHAPTER 7

Capitaine Adinian is incoming.

Stripped down to his T-shirt, he sports enough muscle to make the young women faint. Pressed to his right shoulder like a rifle, he carries a massive drill with its muzzle pointing straight up.

Next to Victor, Chantal's intern Mona fans herself. "Is it me, or is there a studmuffin outside walking in slo-mo like a badass movie hero?"

"Definitely not just you," Sandrine says. "Can you hear the bass and drums crescendo in the background?"

Mona gasps. "Totally!"

Victor cups his ear, but he still can't hear anything.

The women burst out laughing.

"Oh my God, that's Capitaine Adinian, isn't it?" Sandrine asks, licking her lips.

Victor purses his mouth. "I wonder if his commandant knows what he's up to."

As Adinian bolts the makeshift platform to the ground with Karl's help, Julie ogles him. Her youngest sister feigns wiping drool off Julie's chin. Julie goes red in the face and looks away.

Meanwhile, the punk and Isnard have gone back to the van. They resurface with armfuls of plywood cutouts. *The sheets from this morning!* Sawed into triangle shapes, the cutouts have an intricate pattern of holes in the middle, slots along the bottom, and hooks along the sides. They are stained with a light, semitransparent pigment. It gives the shapes a rich green color without hiding its woody vibe.

This is an act of civil disobedience with two gendarmes participating to boot!

The rebels—because that's what they are—fix some of the larger cutouts to the pallet stand and begin to assemble the rest. To Victor's astonishment, most pieces fit together perfectly. The few times a piece refuses to slide in, the punk sands a slot or two, and voilà, in it goes!

Before Victor's incredulous eyes, a big green inverted cone is rising into the sky.

The onlookers film the genesis of the tree with their phones. They cheer and call their friends. Soon, the area is packed with people. From where he's sitting, Victor can't even see much anymore.

Sharply, he sets his fork and knife on the table and storms out of the restaurant.

Jostling his way through the throng, he asks himself if he should order that the unauthorized object be removed immediately.

How would Adinian react? How would the public react? Would they hiss and boo at him? Would they shift into full mutineer mode and squeeze him out of the Place de la Mairie?

Would Adinian execute his order?

He could always call Commandant Lambert…

Victor sweeps a hand over his face and his balding skull. Banning the Christmas tree for environmental reasons was one thing. But bulldozing an eco-friendly substitute built by the town's homeless from reclaimed wood is quite another.

It won't make him look good, no matter how you slice it. Beldocians will hate him. They'll call him the Antichrist. They won't vote for him on election day.

Conflicted, Victor stops a few meters away from the gang of renegades and watches the inverted cone grow taller.

Rose is behind this!

He recalls how he overheard Veronique tell the punk that Rose had an idea "for the other thing." Or something along those lines. This is that other thing!

Victor must admit it was a genius plan. As his challenger, she'll be able to use it in her campaign and position herself as the Woman Who Saved Christmas.

Did I underestimate her? Did I miscalculate so badly, me, a seasoned politician?

Victor believes that all politicians fall into one of three groups—snobs, flatterers, and the real deal.

The snobs and flatterers share the assumption that people are dumb until proven otherwise. To their credit, the snobs are honest enough to not hide from Everyman how little they think of them.

The flatterers pander to conceal their true feelings, but their insincerity shows through sooner or later. In the end, people call their BS because most can tell calculated flattery from genuine respect.

The real deal politicians see their constituents as equals, if not in achievement then in potential. They know how people think. They're authentic, and the masses instinctively trust them.

Victor always saw himself as the real deal.

But now he has doubts.

Has he lost touch with reality? Can he still read the room? Is he mistaken about his constituency's true wants and needs, about who they are? How much does Christmas really mean to them? More than abiding by the law, which, in this case, is their mayor's decree?

Do they love having its symbol, the Christmas tree, more than not having it, which was supposed to stand for their commitment to saving the planet?

The tallest of the rebels—Adinian and the punk—climb on

the tree stand and reach on tiptoe to add the final pieces to their creation.

Lo and behold, Beldoc has a Christmas tree!

Veronique opens her duffel bag and pulls out a roll of fairy lights. The punk threads the end of the wire through a hole at the base of the tree. When the first little bulb goes through, he gives Veronique a delighted grin, suddenly looking more like a ten-year-old than a twenty-year-old.

She claps her hands. "You're a genius!"

They continue to string the lights through the predrilled holes. Julie and the youngest Cavallo girl open their bags wide, and invite the children in the public to help them decorate the tree. A dozen overeager underage volunteers join the insurgency. Together, they hang shiny colorful glass balls on the little hooks and drape gold foil garlands around the tree.

The punk flicks a toggle switch, and the fairy lights come alive with a warm, joyous glow.

The crowd is ecstatic. They clap and cheer. Families and youngsters take group selfies. The older, more dignified citizens just gaze at the tree and smile, their eyes glistening. Karl sniffles and blows his nose.

"Your idea, Capitaine?" someone calls from the crowd. "Is this a gift from the gendarmerie?"

"Only the plywood." Adinian points to the punk. "The rest is him."

A chorus of applause, bravos, and hip hip hurrays ensue.

The punk smiles sheepishly and fidgets, not knowing what to do with his hands or where to look. It's undeniable that the kid has skills. He should be a carpenter, instead of wasting away his life as he does!

Someone intones "Petit Papa Noël," and in the next instant, a DIY Christmas choir is singing their hearts out around the DIY Christmas tree.

"Doesn't this melt your heart, Victor?" Chantal whispers in his ear.

He refuses to answer her question.

"Doesn't it remind you of your childhood?" she persists. "Doesn't it bring back happy memories?"

"My parents were radical deconstructivists. They didn't celebrate Christmas."

"That explains a lot about you," she says.

"Are you going to pull a Clothilde on me?" He turns to her. "Are you going to betray me like she did and switch to Rose's side?"

"Never!" Chantal gives him a genuinely horrified look. "I'm loyal, Victor. How can you doubt me after all these years of working together?"

He nods, reassured. "Forgive me. It was an unfair thing to say. I'm too rattled. It's this Christmas tree—"

"Please don't ruin it, Victor!"

He inhales noisily but keeps his mouth sealed.

Chantal speaks again, "Considering the year we've had, the town needs it more than ever." She glances at the tree and smiles. "It gives us hope."

CHAPTER 8

I t's one week to Christmas.

Victor calls it a day and crosses the bustling Place de la Mairie on his way to the dry cleaner's. He walks past the DIY Christmas tree, which he begrudgingly authorized, to the townsfolk's delight.

As every day, children and grown-ups take selfies and sing carols around the sparkling tree. They were never so enthusiastic about the real, beautiful Christmas tree Beldoc always had. It's as if his ban made them appreciate it more.

Victor had hoped for a good downpour or a return of the mistral to rid him of that troublesome artifact. But no dice.

A miracle! he hears Chantal in his head.

He counters with science. On average, Beldoc gets no more than ten days of rain in December. *So, no, not a miracle,* he tells the imaginary Chantal.

Like every year, Victor is the voice of reason amid collective hysteria. That's what Christmastime is—a bout of madness to which the gullible segment of the population succumbs from November through December. Like the seasonal flu if you will.

In Provence, this period of collective insanity is called *La Calendale.* Other regions and countries may have their own names for it, but the nature of the psychosis remains the

41

same. People stock up on presents, lie to themselves that they give a damn, and see miracles everywhere.

To Victor personally, Christmas is just something he ignores as his parents always did. While Marlene was still part of the Jacquet household, she used to celebrate it in secret. Sometimes Victor caught her praying silently, eyes shut and lips moving. Other times, he'd hear her chant softly in her room when she thought no one else was home.

He disapproved fervently of Marlene's worship, but he never snitched on her. Reporting her illicit prayers to Maman and Papa would've been a shabby, dishonorable move. It felt like something a Nazi collaborator would do when they overheard the neighbor listening to the exiled de Gaulle on *Radio Londres*.

At the dry cleaner's, Victor gets an apology as the expert *teinturier* hands him his favorite beret. To his dismay, the man was unable to restore it to a condition in which it can be worn again.

Darn it!

Trudging home with the forever ruined beret in his hands, Victor realizes how much he'd hoped to wear it again. The more he'd thought about Alex, the more he regretted not having given their relationship his best effort. Gradually, he came to believe it deserved a second chance.

But now, without the beret, he can't do it the easy way.

Victor pulls out his phone and finds Alex's cell number, which he'd never deleted from his contacts. He taps Call.

"Victor?" she says. She sounds a little too surprised for someone who initiated the retry.

They exchange civilities.

He clears his throat. "I've been thinking about you lately."

There's a silence on the other end.

He halts under a tree and leans his forehead on its rough trunk. *This can't be good.*

"I've been thinking about you, too," she says.

Wait, what?

"Are you still single?" he asks bluntly, too stressed to play games.

"I am," she says. "And you?"

"Me, too."

"You were still heartbroken over your wife when we dated four years ago." He hears a rustling sound, like she's sitting down. "You were nowhere near ready to move on."

"I'll always grieve for her, but I believe I'm ready to be with someone new now."

"Listen," she says. "We didn't give ourselves a fighting chance before we drifted apart. If we do this again, let's take it slow. Let's be just friends for a while so we don't feel the pressure."

"Alex, that's an excellent suggestion! I second it wholeheartedly."

"Good." He can hear the smile in her voice. "I'm going to spend the next two weeks in Dublin, with my daughter. She married an Irishman two months ago."

"Congratulations! When you're back, can I take you to lunch or dinner?"

"Let's start with a lunch," she says.

"Deal. You live in Beldoc now, right?"

"No, I'm still in Arles. Why?"

Hmm… How was she supposed to see if he was wearing his checkered beret?

She tee-hees. "Does the distance scare you? It's only a twenty-minute drive for me. Forty for you on your bike. And you can always take the bus."

"No, no, the distance is not a problem at all!" He pauses, choosing his words. "That note you slipped into my mailbox—"

"What note? What are you talking about, Victor?"

"Nothing. It's not important," Victor says, deciding not to press the matter further.

She wishes him a merry Christmas. He wishes her happy holidays. They hang up.

Was her confusion about the note genuine? It sure sounded so. But if she didn't write it, then who did? Who is Alex D?

Or was she simply too embarrassed to admit her authorship of the missive? After all, his direct phone call had turned the beret code into a silly shtick.

As Victor ponders the question, his phone rings. He answers it.

"We need to talk," Rose says. "It's important."

"You want to rub your Christmas tree success in my face, is that it?"

"No," she says in an uncharacteristically grave tone.

"All right, whatever. Come by my office tomorrow."

"Are you already at home?" she asks.

"No, I'm on my way. Why?"

"We're in that little café on the corner of your street. Why don't you stop by?"

"Who's 'we'?"

"My granddaughters Veronique and Julie are here with me," she says.

Whatever for? Then again, the café is on his way, and it's not like he has things to do tonight besides laundry and dishes.

"I'll be there in five minutes," he says and ends the call.

When he joins her in the café, he expects the sisters to take their leave, but they don't budge.

"First off," Rose says, "I want to propose a truce for the rest of *La Calendale.*"

She unpins the Rose for Mayor badge from her sweater and drops it in her purse. Julie and Veronique do the same.

"Oh please, save your grand gestures!" Victor pulls a face. "You're going to take credit for the Christmas tree. And why wouldn't you? I know it was your idea."

Rose puffs out her chest. "And I'm very proud of it!"

"I'm curious, how did you get all those pieces to fit together so well?" He smirks. "You were a PE teacher, not a math teacher."

She lifts an eyebrow. "I opened the computer, googled a pattern, uploaded the scalable PF and—"

"Downloaded the PDF," Julie prompts.

"Right, downloaded the PDF and printed it out." She beams. "I have a printer now!"

"Congrats, it was a brilliant move to get votes," Victor concedes.

"I have no clue how you figured it out, but no one knows it was my idea," Rose says. "There's a reason I didn't show up for the assembling fun."

Victor knits his brows. "Who takes credit for it then? Your granddaughters? Capitaine Adinian?"

"Alex, of course," Julie says. "He's the one who made it happen. He transformed those intricate paper patterns into plywood cutouts using a basic chainsaw. That boy has hands of gold."

Victor freezes up, unable to form words.

"Also Karl," Veronique corrects her sister. "We've been telling everyone that those two came up with the plywood tree idea. Karl has since received a barely worn wool coat and an expensive backpack."

Julie laughs. "And his coin cup has been fuller than ever before!"

At last, Victor finds his tongue. "Alex… the punk?"

CHAPTER 9

"The very same," Julie says.

Victor leans in. "What's his last name?"

"Dubois, I think." Julie glances at Veronique who nods.

Alex D.

The first thing that crosses his mind—that would cross any man's mind—is that young Alex is a son of his. A fruit of a dalliance, whose existence his mother had hidden from Victor during all this time.

Except, Victor never had a dalliance. Solange became his wife twenty-seven years ago. He was unwaveringly faithful to her throughout their long and happy marriage. And as for the two or three short-lived relationships he had before Solange, the punk is much too young to be a product of one of those.

"It's impossible," he mutters under his breath.

The sisters exchange a confused look.

"Never mind." He flashes them a canned smile before turning to Rose. "So, you want me to believe you'll pass on a golden opportunity to be the hero who saved the day?"

"Yes," she says earnestly. "What we did, all together, wasn't about politics. I won't use it for political gain."

He wants to believe her, but his life experience tells him not to.

Rose extends a hand. "Consider it my Christmas present to you, Victor. Maybe, in exchange, you could admit—privately—that your ban was a mistake."

"Never! It was the responsible, eco-friendly thing to do."

She pulls her hand back. "Up until last month, you didn't care about the environment. Then you recast yourself as green, but on the inside you're still red, still a Bolshevik."

"Radical deconstructivist! There's a big difference—"

"Does it matter?" she interrupts him. "You're green now."

His lip curls. "Hey, you too repainted yourself green, I hear."

"From what color?" she asks, arching an eyebrow.

His eyes dart to her lipstick. "From pink!"

"And what political current would that be, pray?" she asks with a smug smile.

"The cheater current," he says. "You've only ever cared about clothes, yoga, and leisure. Your green sovereignist movement? Please! We both know you're only trying to get elected so you can settle your credit card debt without selling your house."

She loses the sneer. "But I do care about nature!"

"As do I!"

They glare at each other for a childishly long amount of time.

"I will never admit the ban was a mistake, but I'll reciprocate your discretion, if you mean it," Victor finds himself saying.

"How?" she asks.

"I'll find the budget to move the urinal to the corner of the street where the sidewalk is wider, and there are no shops or restaurants."

Rose cocks her head.

He shrugs. "Consider it an olive branch I'm extending to Magda." He glances at Julie. "And to you, too, given that your shop is next door."

"Thank you so much!" Julie says.

He turns back to Rose. "But remember, I'll fight you with all I've got once our truce is over."

"I count on it!" she blows him a kiss.

Setting a few coins on the table, he moves to stand up.

Veronique clutches his hand. "Wait!"

Victor sits back. "What now?"

"I must tell you something," she says. "Something personal."

You know a plausible Alex D?

"What can you possibly tell me?" Victor snaps, more at his budding obsession than at Veronique.

"There's a cache in your house where your late wife hid something that wasn't hers," Veronique says. "Something you need to see."

It takes him a good minute to process what he just heard. "And I'm supposed to believe that nonsense?" He fidgets with the beret in his hands. "Are you a psychic or something?"

"I'm not," she says with an awkward smile. "I just had this crazy daydream—a vision—and I'm passing it on to you. I have no idea why I had it, why it was about you, and what it means."

With a sigh, he stands up. "Have a good evening, ladies."

"The cache is in an antique mahogany chest of drawers," Veronique says. "The middle drawer has a false bottom. Will you check it?"

He tightens the grip on his beret. "I will do no such thing. It's ridiculous!"

Veronique gives him a dazed look. "Wait, does it mean there really is an antique mahogany chest in your house? Are you confirming what I saw?"

"Half of all houses have a chest like that, handed down from a grandparent." He squeezes the beret. "Goodbye. I'm out of here."

As he flounces out, he hears Veronique say to the others. "I did it. I told him what I saw. Now it's up to him."

"I'm sure he'll look, and he won't find anything," Rose says. "Your so-called vision was just a vivid dream caused by jet lag."

THE FIRST THING Victor does when he gets home is to pull out the middle drawer of Solange's chest of drawers. Next, he grabs a screwdriver and pries up the bottom.

There is another bottom underneath.

And two unopened letters.

His hands shaking, Victor picks them up and checks the addressee and the sender. They're for him. From Marlene.

He sags against the side of the chest and stays there for a while, coming to terms with what just happened. Then he tears the envelopes open, pulls the letters out and starts with the older one.

Marlene penned it sixteen years ago. It's very short.

I left the monastery.

Hold up, she did? But she was there seven years back when Maman was on her deathbed and he called her convent. How does that compute?

I have a job in Tours now. I met someone and fell in love. We're married now. We have a wonderful baby boy.

Victor stares at the wall, his mind churning. Then he reads the rest.

I'm sending you a picture of the three of us. You can show it to Maman and Papa. I'll be happy to see all of you again.

Love,
Marlene

Victor picks up the envelope and gropes inside. There's the photo! In it, Marlene holds in her arms a fat-cheeked boy, aged two or three. The toddler looks a lot like the man in the picture with his arm around Marlene's shoulders.

Victor rakes his hands through his scant hair before reading the second letter.

In that one, Marlene regrets she didn't get a reply from him or from their parents. She says she won't bother them again. They are happy together and that's enough. If being rejected by her kin is the cross God has given her, then she'll bear it without complaint.

But she'll sin by lying to her son. She'll tell him that cutting her parents and her brother was her decision, that she demanded they stay away from her and her son. She doesn't want Alex to grow up with the wound of being rejected by his family.

An hour passes before Victor can formulate his first coherent thought.

Solange intercepted Marlene's letters and hid them from him. She didn't read them. She didn't destroy them, either. What she did instead was hide them, hoping that after two attempts Marlene will get the message and stop badgering Victor.

But didn't she fear Marlene would call him and ask about the letters?

Maybe she did. Maybe then she would've come clean. Or maybe she would've denied any wrongdoing and blamed the postal service. Whatever the case, Solange's aversion for Marlene's beliefs was so great that she decided for Victor.

She had no right!

Victor resents his sister's obsession with Jesus just as much as Solange did, but she's still family. And, for a time at least, she had quit nunhood! If Victor had received her initial letter, he would've shown it to Maman and Papa, and then jumped on the first train to Tours.

The thought that swoops into his mind next is even more shattering than the previous one.

I have a nephew.

The punk, who must be eighteen or nineteen now, is Marlene's son, Alex Dubois. He's in Beldoc, reaching out to Victor in a clumsy, insecure, typically adolescent way.

And getting rejected by a beret.

CHAPTER 10

Victor's plan was to find Alex first thing in the morning. But the idea that the kid will spend another night thinking his uncle is knowingly ignoring him was too distressing to bear.

At ten in the evening, Victor hightails it to the squat.

The apartment occupied by the punks is easy to find. It's the only one with lights on behind the grimy Plexiglas panels replacing the broken glass. Victor climbs the stairs to the third floor. Once on the landing, identifying the door is just as easy thanks to the loud voices, laughter, and music.

He knocks, gently at first, then louder so the squatters would hear him.

A young man with dreadlocks opens the door. "We're allowed to be here."

"I know," Victor says.

The man's stance relaxes. "How can I help you, monsieur?"

"I just wanted to talk with one of the occupants, Alex Dubois." Victor peeks in trying to spot Alex. "He reached out to me."

"Alex isn't here," the man says.

"Do you know where he is?"

"He's helping a guy named Zorg move to a new house in exchange for pizzas, drinks, and er... smokes for all of us."

Victor stares into the man's eyes. "Zorg?"

"I know, right?" The man grins. "Definitely not his real name."

"When do you expect him back?"

"Actually, he was supposed to be back by eight with the pizzas and everything."

"Has he called?"

The man shakes his head.

"Did you call him?" Victor asks.

"I accidentally dropped my phone in the river yesterday."

Victor inhales slowly. "Has anyone else in the squat talked to him?"

The man turns toward the room. "Guys! Who's had a word from Alex?"

"I left him a message that we're hungry," someone calls from behind a filthy screen. "He never called back."

"Can you try again?" Victor shouts into the room.

"We have." A lad with a ring in his nose comes forward. "It goes straight to voice mail."

Victor's stomach knots with worry. "Will you give me his number so I can try?"

The lad with the nose ring hesitates.

"I'm his uncle, Victor Jacquet," Victor says. "He might be in danger."

He shows the kid his ID.

The kid inspects Victor's ID, then glances at the guy with dreadlocks. "Alex never mentioned an uncle..."

I wouldn't, either, in his shoes. "Did he tell you much about the rest of his family?"

They both shake their heads. "He doesn't like to talk about his folks."

Small wonder!

"It's our fault," Victor says. "Some of us have lied to him, others have snubbed him, albeit unwittingly... We haven't been that great."

The guy with the dreadlocks gives the lad with the nose ring a nod, and the latter pulls up Alex's number. Victor keys it into his phone along with the kid's number. They say goodbye, promising to keep each other informed.

The second he's outside, Victor calls Alex, and gets his voice mail. Next, he phones Beldoc's top gendarme. It's rude to call people this late, but this is an emergency.

Commandant Lambert takes the time to hear Victor out. Better still, he pings Capitaine Adinian who's on duty tonight. Adinian calls Victor back immediately. They agree to meet at the gendarmerie in fifteen minutes.

When Victor gets to the gendarmerie, breathless, Capitaine Adinian and *Caporal* Isnard are waiting by their blue Renault Mégane. Its doors are open.

Adinian points to the back seat. "Jump in, Monsieur le Maire."

Isnard takes the wheel. Adinian climbs into the front passenger seat.

As they peel out, Adinian sticks a flashing beacon on the roof.

The car radio crackles. "Are you en route?"

Adinian confirms before looking over his shoulder at Victor. "We used geolocation to find Alex's cell phone. He's moving fast. Must be inside a vehicle, headed east."

They race toward the signal for the next twenty minutes, steadily catching up. Victor's heart beats at a tempo that matches Isnard's speed.

"We'll be neck and neck in less than five minutes," Adinian says.

"Did Commandant Lambert tell you I'm Alex's uncle?" Victor asks him.

"Yes."

"I had no idea until two hours ago."

"You'll get a chance to explain that to him," Adinian says. "He's a great kid. He'll understand."

Victor rubs his temples with the balls of his hands. "I hope so."

The dispatcher in the radio says, "Capitaine, the signal stopped moving. And now… it died."

"Gives us the exact coordinates," Adinian responds, keeping his voice calm.

Five minutes later, they pull over by the edge of the woods. Adinian calls in backup. The three of them get out of the car. Isnard and Adinian turn on their flashlights and run off into the woodland. Victor scrambles behind them.

"Backup will be here soon," Adinian says to him, directing Isnard toward the left while he veers to the right. "They'll help us comb the area."

Victor trips on a tree root but manages not to fall. "What does this mean, Capitaine? Please, be honest with me! Do you expect him to be… to be…"

"We focus on the search now," Adinian says. "Stay close and keep your eyes open."

His cell phone rings. Adinian's eyebrows rise when he glances at the caller ID. He picks up.

Victor can hear a female voice, but he can't make out what she's saying.

Adinian listens, his expression focused and, at the same time, skeptical.

"Victor Jacquet is here with me," he says. "I'll put you on speaker."

He holds his phone closer to Victor.

"Monsieur le Maire," Julie says, "I just explained to Capitaine Adinian that Vero saw—Oh, by the way, did you check that drawer?"

"I did," he says. "And she was right, although I'm sure there's a rational explanation for it. But this is not the right time."

"Veronique here," Julie's sister takes over. "You're right, there's no time. I'll get straight to the point. I saw three youths, two male and a female, unmoving, in the cargo area of a truck."

"How exactly did you see them?" Victor asks.

"In my mind."

Under normal circumstances, Victor would end the call right there. But he's desperate. "Was Alex one of them?"

"Yes."

Adinian lowers his head toward the phone. "Was the truck still or was it moving?"

"It was moving," she says.

"How big was it?"

"Quite big."

"What shape, what color?" Adinian asks.

"Regular freight truck shape, tall and long, white."

Adinian glances at Victor. "Every second freight truck on the road matches that description."

"Wait, it had stripes on its side…" There's a brief silence as if Veronique is trying to recollect the particulars. "Green, white, and red."

"That's Italy," Adinian says.

"Inside the cargo area," Veronique continues, "there's a wall of cardboard boxes between the youths and the tailgate. Floor to ceiling, many layers of them. Different types of pasta. Spaghetti, tortellini, fusilli, linguine, fettuccine—"

"I get the picture," Adinian interrupts her. "Anything else? Could you hear anything?"

Another silence, then Veronique says, "I'm afraid not. I'm sorry."

"That's all right," Adinian says. "Thank you for your help, madame! I appreciate it."

He ends the call and turns to Victor. "I don't know why I kept pressing her for details. It's not like I took any of it seriously."

"I myself don't believe in that sort of stuff," Victor says. "But…"

How to tell this down-to-earth cop that Veronique's earlier tip-off turned out to be correct?

Cautiously, he begins again, "I know that some police and gendarmerie units have resorted to mediums to help them find missing persons."

"Some do," Adinian says. "But the vast majority of

mediums are con artists. The few who aren't may sincerely believe they have a gift. They act in good faith thinking they can help the investigators, but typically, they're wrong, and a nuisance, and a cause of much wasted time."

"Listen, Capitaine, I agree. I'm a materialist, and I've never believed in such things. But…"

Adinian squints at him.

Victor rolls his shoulders. "If there is, perhaps, 1 percent of so-called psychics who, maybe, sometimes, inadvertently, get it right, then Veronique is one of them."

"You sound like you believe her," Adinian says, frowning.

"I do, and I have a good reason for it."

For a split second Adinian appears ready to object, or to ask a question, but then his expression changes. "It's true that the gendarmerie never ignores a medium's call, since our policy is to take all reports seriously. There's a special unit to which we refer the psychics' reports."

"What does that unit do?"

"They process the info and compare it with the details on file," Adinian says. "Sometimes, when the report seems credible, they follow up."

Victor nods. He's on the same page as Adinian—a realist and a skeptic. Referring a psychic's insight to a dedicated unit is the best way to deal with it. So what if Veronique was right about the letters? She could've come by that information in a perfectly normal way, through someone.

"Personally, I've never had a reliable tip from a psychic," Adinian adds, as if he is trying to convince himself that he's making the right call. "And I've never heard of a psychic solving a missing person case."

Victor nods again.

And then he finds himself asking, "Can we follow up on Veronique's intel? Right now, before the trail goes cold?"

Strictly speaking, it wasn't a request. It was a plea.

Adinian stares at Victor for a few seconds and then calls Caporal Isnard. "Have you heard from the backup units?"

"They're already here, *mon Capitaine*, combing the woods," Isnard responds.

"Go back to the car. We're going to follow a new lead." Adinian turns to Victor and shrugs. "Let's go. I'm assessing Veronique's report as credible. You better be right about her!"

CHAPTER 11

"Where to, Capitaine?" Isnard asks as they buckle up.

"Before we lost the signal," Adinian says, "It was moving eastward, maybe to Italy. Let's assume the truck hasn't changed course."

Isnard presses on the gas. *"Oui, mon Capitaine!"*

Victor tries to imagine what happened. "Alex's kidnappers must've stopped where we lost the signal. They took his phone into the woods and smashed it there to send any potential search party on a wild-goose chase."

"It's possible," Adinian says.

While Victor keeps his eyes on the road, hoping to spot a white truck, Adinian radios the gendarmerie. "Can you check if a young man and a young woman have been reported missing in the area lately?"

"On it!"

"One other thing," Adinian says to the dispatcher. "Ask all road patrols in Bouches du Rhône, Var and Alpes Maritimes to look out for a white truck with green, white and red stripes on the side. If they see one, they must escort it to the nearest truck scanner."

"What are we looking for?" the dispatcher asks.

"Human stowaways in the cargo area behind boxes of

pasta," Adinian says. "It's a suspected kidnapping. Possibly three victims, young, two male, one female. They may be unconscious or dead."

Isnard glances at Adinian. "Organ trafficking? Forced prostitution rings?"

"Alex told me he was clean, barring an occasional joint or beer," Adinian says. "Maybe he'd also shared that info with the guy who trapped him. He makes for a perfect candidate—away from home, transient, young, and healthy."

They drive along the A8 for an hour, stop two Italian trucks, have them scanned, find nothing.

The wait is excruciating.

A powerful emotion Victor hasn't experienced since Solange's passing takes hold of him.

When she was diagnosed, he wished he could swap places with her. If someone in their household had to have leukemia, then he'd rather it be him than her. It was an utterly irrational urge that went against his self-interest, survival instinct, and sense of self-preservation.

He feels the same way now about his nephew whose existence he didn't about until a few hours ago. The thought that the kid might be dead is breaking his heart.

Dear Lord, if someone in my family has to die tonight, let it be me!

Victor startles at the wish he just formed. Was that a prayer? It couldn't've been. He wouldn't've done that. Even in Solange's worst moments, he didn't pray because what's the point? To pray, one must believe in the existence of the heavenly overlord. Victor doesn't, never did, never will.

His "Dear Lord" was just a figure of speech. Nothing more.

Adinian asks the dispatcher to warn the Italian police in case the truck gets there before the French patrols can catch it. He seems to be acting on the assumption that Veronique's information was good. Victor knows he doesn't actually think that, and he feels grateful to the capitaine for trusting him on this.

In the wee hours of the morning, Isnard and Adinian drop Victor off with the promise to call him the second they hear something.

Victor thanks them and drags himself into his suddenly cold and empty home.

The call comes a mere forty minutes later.

With shaking hands Victor answers the phone.

VICTOR and his sister Marlene are in the waiting area of the Joseph Imbert Hospital in Arles. They haven't talked much since Victor called the monastery this morning and gave her the news about Alex. She arrived in Arles by five in the afternoon. They met in the lobby of the hospital for the first time in thirty-four years.

Victor sneaks a look at Marlene. She's still as thin as she was when she skipped town—unlike Victor who filled out— but her face has lost all its youthful smoothness and glow.

She isn't wearing a nun's habit. Victor wonders if she was allowed to take it off and leave the convent because this is an emergency or if she was obliged to quit nunhood again to come out here. But those questions can wait.

Right now, they both have their eyes peeled on the door where Alex is expected to emerge, once his checkup is complete.

Victor already told Marlene what he'd learned from Adinian.

Alex had been heavily sedated by his captors. After dark, he was driven to a freight truck park outside Beldoc and shoved into a truck. The other two youths were already in there, drugged.

Somewhere between Salon and Aix, the mobsters realized they'd forgotten to pat Alex down. They exited the highway, found his phone, took it into the woodland by the road and smashed it there.

The backup team Adinian had called in found the remains of that phone, by the way.

Then the kidnappers hit the road again, driving east to Italy. A patrol near Cannes stopped them, based on Adinian's description. The mobile X-ray scanner showed a suspicious presence that was confirmed by a dog sweep. The gendarmes unloaded the pasta boxes and found three unconscious youths. "Zorg" and his accomplice were taken into custody.

The door opens, and the eagerly awaited doctor comes out, smiling. She steps aside to let Alex step out.

The kid had been told that his mom and uncle were

waiting outside, so he doesn't seem surprised to see them. Not that he actually looks at them. Alex stops and keeps his eyes down, all sharp elbows, skinny hips and clumsy feet. He has dark circles under his eyes. His green mohawk is all mussed up.

Marlene throws her arms around him. "My baby! You gave me such a scare! Have you been in Beldoc all this time? Why did you tell me you were in Lyon?"

"You would've been mad," he says.

"No, of course not!" She pulls away to look into his eyes. "Oh, God, is that what you thought?"

Victor turns to the doctor. "How is he doing?"

"Great," she says. "Alex and the other two were drugged so they would sleep through their kidnapping, but they suffered no physical harm."

"It stands to reason." Victor grimaces. "Those bastards needed the kids in good condition."

She nods before turning to Alex. "Lots of water over the next few days and take it easy, all right?"

"I will, *Docteur*."

"Have the gendarmes questioned you already?" Victor asks Alex.

"Yes," he says. "Capitaine Adinian said he'll need to ask a few more questions later, but for now he had enough to go on."

The doctor motions toward the corridor. "Let me take you to the discharge desk."

CHAPTER 12

Two hours later, the three of them are walking the festive streets of Beldoc.

Marlene is deeply moved to be back in her childhood town.

Victor is a little emotional, too. For the first time this winter—and the first time in his adult life—he looks at the Christmas decorations and likes them. All of them. The sparkling lights strung up between buildings, the shimmery deer on front lawns, and even the tacky Santas climbing into windows.

How odd!

They reach Place de la Mairie and make their way through the market to the chestnut stand manned by Karl. Victor notes with satisfaction that Karl hasn't deserted his post yet. Granted, this is no guarantee that he'll find—or agree to take—another job once the Christmas market is gone. But it's the first time in a decade that Karl has held a job for more than a day.

Alex gives him a bear hug, startling Karl who knows nothing of the ordeal the kid has been through over the past twenty-four hours.

The dog stands on its hind paws and scrapes Alex's thighs, tail wagging fiercely as if to say, *Me too, hug me too*!

Alex lets go of Karl and hunkers down. "Hey, Harley, old boy! I'm so happy to see you!"

Harley puts his front paws around Alex's neck and licks his cheek while Alex pets him.

"Who's the chestnut man?" Marlene whispers in Victor's ear.

Victor tells her about Karl, and how the hobo took care of Alex when he turned up in Beldoc before he found the punks and their squat.

Alex finally stands up. Victor leads his sister and nephew toward Le Grand Comptoir. While Marlene and Alex were talking on the bus from Arles, he called the restaurant and booked a dinner table. But before they can get to it, they must elbow their way through the packed circle around the DIY Christmas tree.

The exercise turns out to be less of a challenge than Victor expected.

Seeing them, people cheer, pat Alex on the back, and clear a path. Not surprising, given that the kid is the artisan behind the tree. What's harder to explain is that the townsfolk greet Victor with smiles and joyous, "Bonjour, Monsieur le Maire!"

How can they be so indulgent, despite his banning of their beloved live Christmas tree? Only a week ago, they were signing in droves the petition to rescind the ban and calling for him to resign!

Victor struggles to understand their forgiveness.

They stop before the DIY tree.

Alex points to the crest that was still bare yesterday. "Look, someone added a star topper!"

Victor asks Marlene, "Has he told you he built that thing?"

She turns to Alex, euphoric. "Really? Is that true?"

"The design wasn't mine. And it doesn't mean I believe in *Père Noël* again!" He gives her a mutinous look, but the toothy grin that comes next shows how stoked he is.

Alex has every reason to be proud.

Even Victor feels pleased and proud on Alex's behalf as his uncle. The feeling fills his chest with warmth.

He points to the restaurant on the left. "We're having dinner there."

Marlene shifts uncomfortably. "It looks expensive."

"Eating in a restaurant is against the punk philosophy," Alex says.

"Oh, shush, both of you!" Victor feigns vexation. "Can you do it for me as a favor? It'll give me so much pleasure!"

His sister and nephew say they can.

Victor is secretly hoping to convince them to stay at his house, at least for the next day or two. But he'll bring that up only after dessert.

Over the apéritif, he learns that Alex's father left them when Alex was six. He went to live abroad and remarried. It's clear he hasn't been in the picture since then, and that it pains Marlene. Not so much for herself as for Alex.

Victor also learns she's no longer a nun. She returned to the convent when Alex was nine, as an oblate, a layperson who is allowed to lead a semi-religious life in a monastery. That explains why she was there seven years ago when Maman died. Who could've thought that in the intervening years she had left, lived a married life, made a baby, and then returned in a new capacity?

As the conversation flows over the starters and main course, Victor realizes things are complicated between mother and son. Alex rejects her faith. She's heartbroken about it. The kid seems to sense there's something she's hiding from him, and it's driven a wedge between them.

Victor knows what it is. *It's time to set the truth free.*

He clears his throat. "Alex, you must've been wondering why it took me so long to respond to your note."

Tensing, Alex shoots him an apprehensive glance.

"Here's the thing, I had no idea the note was from you," Victor says. "Until yesterday, I had no clue you existed."

"I knew it!" Alex glowers at Marlene. "You didn't just cut all ties and tell your folks to stay away. You never told them about me!"

Her objection is surprisingly quiet. "It's not true."

"Your mother did tell us," Victor says to Alex. "She sent me two letters. And a sweet picture of you as a toddler."

Alex fidgets, eyebrows knit. "I don't understand."

"Those letters never reached me," Victor says. "My late wife, Solange, intercepted and hid them. I found them yesterday."

They eat their desserts in silence while Marlene and Alex process what he just told them.

When they're done, Victor offers them a place to stay for a few days. He insists, shamelessly playing the "I've already been deprived of the first eighteen years of my nephew's life!" card.

Marlene and Alex say yes, but only for two days, and please, not a word to Alex's squat roomies! They'll call him a sellout!

Which reminds Alex that his roomies haven't heard from him since yesterday morning. He borrows Victor's phone and darts out to make a call.

Victor turns to Marlene. "So, you quit nunhood for good, huh? I like that! Tell me, do you still believe Jesus died for our sins and was then resurrected?"

"Of course! I never stopped."

He lets out a sigh. "Fine. You're free to believe in miracles if it brings you comfort."

Marlene looks at Victor for a long moment without uttering a word.

Her eyes glisten when she finally speaks. "This Christmas brought me so much more than comfort, Victor! Alex and I can mend our relationship now because I won't be lying to him anymore." She touches his hand. "And you reentered my life."

And you, mine. Both of you.

Victor pulls her into his embrace. While they sit like that, hugging like two old fools, he wonders if Christmas really gives people hope that things will get better. Does it remind them that difficulties can be overcome and that, at the end of the day, good will triumph over evil? Is there really more to it than consumerism?

Can he concede to Clothilde and to pretty much everyone around him that Christmas is also about family and friendship, connectedness, and love?

Marlene lets go of him and wipes her wet face with a napkin. He takes in the little wrinkles around her mouth, the white strands in her hair, her modest clothing. The happiness in her eyes.

Alex saunters back in, hands Victor his phone, and plonks himself down. "I'll crash at your place one night only, Uncle Vic. My buds and the punk lifestyle are very important to me. I hope you understand."

"I do, and to prove it, I'll send you back with pizzas for your friends."

"Cool!" Alex high-fives him. "But it'll be a one-off. Or else they'll call me a trust fund punk."

Victor feigns shock. "That would be a terrible insult, given your pedigree of reds and nuns!"

Right there and then, Mayor Victor Jacquet decides he can do it. He can concede to Clothilde that what she said about Christmas was not entirely wrong.

THE MAYOR WHO CANCELED CHRISTMAS

Julie has her freedom,
a dream job as a pastry chef,
and a corpse growing cold on her floor...

Welcome to Beldoc, a small town in the heart of Provence, imbued with lavender and fresh baked bread! You can idle around, or you can puzzle out a murder mystery.

When a man dies on her watch in her pâtisserie, newly divorced chef Julie Cavallo is dismayed.
It isn't that she's a suspect.
The local gendarmerie captain signs off the death as a natural event. A heart attack.
But for a reason she won't discuss, Julie suspects Maurice Sauve was poisoned.
What's a girl to do?
She'll ignore the risk and seek justice for Maurice on her own!

Well, not quite on her own. Julie's eccentric grandmother, her snarky sister and her geeky sous chef are keen to help.
The team's amateurism is a challenge.
But there's also the pesky matter of no evidence, no clues, and soon, no body.
The murder—if it was a murder—was planned and executed flawlessly.

Can a small-town baker solve the perfect crime?

Get your copy now!

Or turn the page to read an excerpt

I hope you enjoyed this Christmas novella!

If you haven't read my Julie Cavallo mysteries yet, here's a sneak peek at book 1, "The Murderous Macaron."

Julie has her freedom,
a dream job as a pastry chef,
and a corpse growing cold on her floor...

Welcome to Beldoc, a small town in the heart of Provence,

imbued with lavender and fresh baked bread! You can idle around, or you can puzzle out a murder mystery.

When a man dies on her watch in her pâtisserie, newly divorced chef Julie Cavallo is dismayed.
It isn't that she's a suspect.
The local gendarmerie captain signs off the death as a natural event. A heart attack.
But for a reason she won't discuss, Julie suspects Maurice Sauve was poisoned.
What's a girl to do?
She'll ignore the risk and seek justice for Maurice on her own!

Well, not quite on her own. Julie's eccentric grandmother, her snarky sister and her geeky sous chef are keen to help.
The team's amateurism is a challenge.
But there's also the pesky matter of no evidence, no clues, and soon, no body.
The murder—if it was a murder—was planned and executed flawlessly.

Can a small-town baker solve the perfect crime?

≈

Turn the page to read an excerpt!

EXCERPT FROM "THE MURDEROUS MACARON"

JULIE CAVALLO INVESTIGATES, BOOK 1

"People drop dead on strangers all the time." Flo gives me an emphatic look. "Stop sulking, it's bad for business. Life goes on, Julie!"

At that, she waves and exits the shop.

Heeding my younger sister's questionable pep talk, I pick up a box of pistachio macarons and begin to gift wrap it.

The front door chimes, announcing a new customer.

I force the corners of my mouth upward in what I hope resembles a professional smile. But my face lengthens again when I realize who's entering the shop. The man in the doorway isn't a customer. He's a cop, Capitaine Gabriel Adinian of the Beldoc Gendarmerie. The one who's looking into the death of Maurice Sauve.

I hug myself, as a sudden shiver runs through my body on this balmy June afternoon.

That poor man!

To go so quickly and irreversibly, and at the worst possible time! Not just from my perspective, even though I can't deny I'd rather he suffered his heart attack before or after my macaron-making class. On a less selfish note, the timing was unfortunate for Maurice himself. When I asked everyone at the beginning of the workshop to tell the class about themselves, he said he'd been through a prolonged midlife crisis and had finally glimpsed the light at the end of the tunnel.

He said he'd embarked on a quest for a purpose to his life after realizing two years back that sorting mail at the post office wasn't it. A year of volunteering with the Red Cross in Southeast Asia convinced him that charity work wasn't it either. Back in Beldoc, he dipped a toe into all sorts of things from music to stock trading. Recently, he discovered baking.

I remember him gushing as he concluded his introduction: "I have a really good feeling about this!"

Twenty minutes later, he grimaced, collapsed to the floor, and died.

I shudder and rub my arms.

As Capitaine Adinian draws nearer, I train my gaze on his face. His features are highly irregular. In theory, no woman would find him handsome unless she'd been studying iguanas on a deserted island for a year.

In actuality, the matter of his attractiveness is less straightforward.

The overall structure of his face makes up for the flaws of his individual features. His prominent nose and mouth match the angular firmness of his jawline, which his three-day-old stubble cannot hide. His dark brown eyes reel you in. He gives off an aura of effortless, natural virility.

Chill out, Julie.

It's just a visceral reaction of a thirty-year-old woman to a guy she finds hot. It'll pass in a moment. Besides, I don't find him hot. And, recalling his attitude during our first encounter last night, I don't even like him.

Capitaine Adinian halts across the counter from me.

A thought crosses my mind. What if this isn't about Maurice Sauve? What if he's come here with the aim of purchasing an assortment of my confections?

Ha-ha. That was the most ridiculous of all the ridiculous ideas I've ever had. And, trust me, I've had many.

Adinian surveys me, muttering something unintelligible under his breath.

I choose to interpret it as "Good morning, Madame Cavallo" and not "You didn't think I was done with you, eh".

The latter option is more likely though. I'm sure Flo would agree. My little sis likes to say that if you keep mentally photoshopping the ugly truth out of people, you'll surround yourself with friends you can always rely on to backstab you. At twenty-two, she's full of acerbic wisdom, aka snark, that she dishes out to all and sundry.

"Julie's Gluten-Free Delights," Adinian says, quoting the sign above the entrance. "But here in Beldoc, we like our gluten."

Is that his idea of a friendly icebreaker? The butterflies in my stomach calm down, as he confirms that he's exactly who I think he is. A discourteous hick.

"I may have lived in Paris half my life"—I look him directly in the eye—"but I'm a Beldocian like you. You'd be surprised how many residents are gluten-intolerant or gluten-sensitive."

Personally, I'm neither. But for the sake of coherence, I stopped consuming wheat-based food the moment I decided to launch a gluten-free bakery.

"Of course," Adinian deadpans.

And then he looks left and right, as if trying to figure out where all those gluten-free buffs might be hiding in my empty shop.

The cheek of him!

I wish Rose was here this morning! She'd flip back her perfect silver bob and arch a masterfully shaped eyebrow. "What happened to good manners, young man?" she'd say in her most la-di-da tone of voice while staring him down. My grandma might even tell him to step out and reenact his entry, politely this time.

And you know what? He just might do it. There's something about Rose that compels people, pets, and potted plants to indulge her.

Eric steps out of the kitchen. "The vanilla macaron shells

are ready, Chef. Want to check before I stick them in the oven?"

"No, that's fine, go ahead," I say to my sous chef before turning back to Capitaine Adinian.

"We're going to conclude natural death," Adinian says, skipping any form of transition.

I give him a small nod.

"Monsieur Sauve's family said he'd been under a lot of stress over the last two years," he adds. "Too much beer, too little exercise. They had feared he'd end up with a heart attack."

"His *family*?" I was under the impression Maurice Sauve was single. Then again, he never said as much.

Adinian puts his elbow on the counter. "He had a cousin living on the same street."

"I see."

He half-turns toward the door, then scratches the back of his head, and turns toward me again. "Can you recount last evening's events again, everything you remember?"

"Er... again? Why?" The prospect of reliving those moments doesn't appeal to me at all. "Didn't you just say there wasn't any foul play involved?"

"It's just formality. I'm finishing my report, and I want to make sure I have all the details right."

My shoulders slump. "OK."

He heads toward the sitting area, plonks himself down into a vintage bistro chair, and points to another chair. "Have a seat."

Making ourselves at home, are we?

Trying not to show my irritation, I sit down across a round table from him and begin my sad tale of yesterday's macaron-making workshop that didn't go as planned.

He listens, barely taking any notes.

When I get to the part where I asked my students to mix the ingredients I'd prepared for them, Capitaine Adinian leans forward. "Who prepared and laid out the ingredients?"

"I did."

76

"When?"

"Shortly before the class began."

"Did you leave the shop, even for a brief time, after you had everything ready for the class?" he asks.

"No."

He scribbles something in his little notebook. "Please continue."

"Most participants struggled to get their batter to stiffen," I say. "Some gave up, claiming it was impossible without an electric mixer."

"Did Maurice Sauve give up?"

"Quite the contrary. He whisked unrelentingly, switching hands but never pausing. He was the first to complete the task."

Capitaine Adinian writes that down.

"I gave him one of these." I show Adinian the remaining badges that Flo had made for the workshop.

"Great Baking Potential," he reads aloud.

"Then I went around with his bowl and had everyone admire the perfect consistency of the batter."

"Did anything stand out or seem unusual at that point?"

I gaze up at the ceiling, picturing the scene of me praising Maurice Sauve's firm, satiny batter, students giving him their thumbs-up, and him smiling, visibly stoked. But he isn't just smiling, he's also… Panic squeezing my throat, I zero in on his face. He's panting.

Oh. My. God.

I clap my hand over my mouth. "What if he'd whisked too hard? What if that exertion caused his heart attack?"

"Only an intense workout, especially at freezing temperatures, can trigger a heart attack," Adinian says.

"He whisked intensely."

"Madame Cavallo, I've never heard of anyone whisking themselves to an early grave."

End of Excerpt

FREE RECIPE BOOK

Did some of the passages in the novel you just finished make you want to bake?

Then sign up for my newsletter and receive a free cookbook in your inbox!

The quick and easy gluten-free recipes in it include:

- macarons
- cookies
- brownies

- tiramisu
- fritters
- puddings

and more!

To sign up, type this url into your browser:
ana-drew.com/patissier

ABOUT THE AUTHOR

Ana T. Drew is the evil mastermind behind the recent series of murders in the fictional French town of Beldoc.

When she is not writing cozy mysteries or doing mom-and-wife things, she can be found watching "The Rookie" to help her get over "Castle".

She lives in Paris but her heart is in Provence.

Website: ana-drew.com

amazon.com/author/ana-drew
facebook.com/AnaDrewAuthor
goodreads.com/anadrew
bookbub.com/authors/ana-t-drew

ALSO BY ANA T. DREW

The Mayor Who Canceled Christmas
(novella)

THE **JULIE CAVALLO INVESTIGATES** SERIES

The Murderous Macaron

The Killer Karma

The Sinister Superyacht

Printed in Great Britain
by Amazon

64580313R00054